MW01178437

# ROAD TO JOY

## A DOGS OF FIRE CHRISTMAS NOVELLA

# PIPER DAVENPORT

Liz
May your road always lead to

Piper ♡ joy!

Piper Davenport

Sale of this book without a front cover may be unauthorized. If this book is coverless, it may have been reported to the publisher as "unsold or destroyed" and neither the author nor the publisher may have received payment for it.

*Road to Joy* is a work of fiction. Names, characters, places, and incidents are the products of the author's imagination and are used fictitiously. Any resemblance to actual events, locales, or persons, living or dead, is entirely coincidental.

## Cover Art
Jackson Jackson

TRIXIE
PUBLISHING

2017 Piper Davenport
Copyright © 2017 by Trixie Publishing, Inc.
All rights reserved.

ISBN-13: 978-1979736237
ISBN-10: 1979736235

Published in the United States

DOGS OF FIRE

PRAISE

*All it took was one page and I was immediately hooked on Piper Davenport's writing. Her books contain 100% Alpha and the perfect amount of angst to keep me reading until the wee hours of the morning. I absolutely love each and every one of her fabulous stories.* ~ Anna Brooks – Contemporary Romance Author

*Get ready to fall head over heels! I fell in love with every single page and spent the last few wishing the book would never end!* ~ Harper Sloan, NY Times & USA Today Bestselling Author

*Piper Davenport just reached deep into my heart and gave me every warm and fuzzy possible.* ~ Geri Glenn, Author of the Kings of Korruption MC Series

*This is one series I will most definitely be reading!! Great job Ms. Davenport!! I am in love!!* ~ Tabitha, Amazeballs Book Addicts

**For my readers**

*May the magic of the season bring joy to you and your families.*

BOOKER & DANI

*Dani*

"**D**ANIELLE HARRIS CARVER!" Austin yelled from the back of the house. "You need to get that sexy ass in the recliner right now."

Austin "Booker" Carver had been my husband for close to ten years, and I loved him more today than I did yesterday, but I still rolled my eyes at his overprotective tone. "Honey, I'm fine. The baby's fine, we're all fine. I need to get these favors done."

"Danielle," he warned.

I was currently standing at my kitchen island (because sitting was way too uncomfortable), and stuffing mini-stockings for all of the neighborhood kids, the Dogs Wolfpack, and any others that might show up to the Dogs of Fire Annual Christmas Party happening the following Saturday. Every year, we collected gifts for Toys for Tots, and then gave any cash donations we received to Bikers Against Child Abuse.

"Kim's going to be here in less than ten minutes... I don't want to leave her a mess to deal with," I said.

My almost nine-year-old, Cash, walked into the middle of the kitchen and crossed his arms. "Mom. You need to listen to Dad." He pointed to the chair. "Go sit down."

I forced myself not to laugh. You'd think I'd never had a baby before.

Granted, this pregnancy was a huge surprise,

considering our youngest, Archer, was almost six and we'd decided we were done after him. But my husband and I fucked like rabbits, so I suppose this was inevitable. On top of that, Austin was raising mini-Bookers and I couldn't wait to have this little girl to even the score a bit.

I turned and stared down my very alpha first-born. "Listen, buddy, I pushed you out of my vagina, and if you want to keep giving me that attitude, I will have no qualms about shoving you back up there. So, how about you give me a break, and either help me with the stockings or empty the dishwasher, hm?"

"Ugh, Mom." He groaned. "Do you have to make everything gross?"

"Yes. It's my job. I gave birth to you so I could embarrass you whenever I got the chance."

"I'll help with the stockings," Archer offered, appearing like an apparition. "Cash can do the dishwasher."

"Both of you can help with the stockings, while Mom sits down," Austin countered as he walked into the room, still pulling on a T-shirt. "Get on those dishes, Cash."

I'd hoped that Austin's shower would take a

little longer, because I had shit to do and he kept stopping me from doing it, but I was thwarted once again. I had about six weeks left and I prayed she didn't come early, because a Christmas birthday sucked for kids and I really didn't want to do that to her.

Austin slid his hands down my hips and kissed the back of my neck. I leaned back against him and settled my hands over his, which were now on my belly. "How's our girl?"

"She's good, honey."

"She'll be better in the chair," he said, and guided me to the recliner.

"Wait," I said. "I have to pee. If I sit down now, I'll never get back up."

"Pee." Austin faced me, kissing me gently. "Then you're in the chair."

I smiled, reaching up to stroke his gorgeous face. "Then I'm in the chair."

He patted my butt, and I headed to the bathroom, returning to the sound of the doorbell. "I'll get it."

"No, you won't," Austin countered. "Ass. In the chair. Now."

I stuck my tongue out at him, but sat my ass in the chair and reclined all the way back.

Archer came over and kissed my cheek, settling a blanket over me. He was my sensitive little prince and was always making sure Mama was taken care of.

"Thank you, baby."

He smiled and joined his brother at the island again to finish the stockings.

"Auntie Dani!" Cambry squealed, and rushed inside. God, she was growing up so fast. She had just turned eight, but she was already a total beauty and I had it on good authority Knight bought a new gun every year on her birthday.

"Watch Auntie's belly, Cam," Kim ordered, and I grinned over at my best friend who was directing while her husband, Knight, and their son, Jagger, set bags in our "staging area" in the dining room.

My niece hugged me. "How's the baby?"

I guided her hand to my belly and grinned. "She must know you're here…she's jumping around."

Cambry giggled. "We have too many boys in the pack, we need more girls."

"Right?" I said.

Knight wrapped his arms around her from

behind and pulled her close. "Give us dads a break, princess. We already have a hard enough time keeping the boys away."

"You said that's why you have guns, Daddy," Cambry said. "Which is silly."

Knight grinned and gave her one more squeeze, before following Austin into the kitchen. Kim gave me a kiss on the cheek, then sat on the sofa next to Cambry.

"How are you feeling, Mama?" she asked.

"Like a whale," I admitted.

Kim smiled. "Well, you look beautiful."

"Thanks, bestie. You're good value."

"I tell you that shit every second of every day, but when Kim says it, she's 'good value'?" Austin complained as he set a cup of tea on the little table by my chair and leaned down to kiss my cheek.

"Where the hell did you come from?" I asked. "You're like a ninja."

"Badass biker ninja," he corrected. "And don't you forget it."

I grinned. "Thank you for the tea."

"You're welcome." He kissed my mouth, then walked back to the kitchen.

"Do you boys need help with the food?" Kim

called out.

"We got it, sugar," Knight responded.

"I love it when he has it." She tucked her feet under her and grinned. "Means I can relax."

I shifted, balancing my teacup and saucer on my belly. "I'm going a little stir-crazy. We have so much to do and Austin won't let me do it."

"Honey, we've got this," Kim assured. "Jesus, Dani, we have almost a dozen women not including you, so it's all good. The men'll do all the heavy lifting…you just need to sit there and look pretty."

"Listen to your bestie, baby," Austin called out.

"Stop eavesdropping," I retorted, and he laughed, leading Knight out to the deck.

"I brought a bunch of Cambry's old clothes," Kim continued. "Want to go through them with me?"

"Ohmigod, yes," I said, and set my teacup on the side table again.

Kim helped me out of the chair, then she and Cambry carried bags (and bags) of clothing into the nursery.

"Oh my gosh, Auntie, this room looks so cool!" Cambry exclaimed.

She was right, it did. Pinks and creams, and lots of blingy, girly things mixed in with motorcycles. It could only be described as biker chic.

I gave Cambry a quick hug. "Thanks, honey. Your mom helped…a *lot*."

"Sit down, Dani," Kim ordered. "Cambry and I'll show you everything and then you can tell us where you want it."

I lowered myself into the recliner and sat in awe of everything Kim had brought. It shouldn't surprise me. Kim was loaded and loved to shop, so her daughter was the best-dressed little girl on the planet, and now my little girl would benefit from her shopping addiction.

"Dad says steaks are done," Cash said from the doorway.

"Thanks, honey," I said. Kim helped me out of the chair and we headed to the dining room.

One of the things I loved the most about my best friend was that she knew my home almost as well as I did, and since I wasn't allowed to lift a finger, Kim took over getting everything set out on the table.

We always tried to do dinner once a month, but tonight was special because it was Jagger's birthday and I'd baked him his favorite cake, banana with chocolate frosting. In pure Jagger fashion, he plowed through dinner just to get to the celebration.

"Boys, dishes rinsed and stacked," Austin ordered, while Kim and I settled ourselves on the sofa. She had wine, I had water (joy).

"Cambry, wipe up, princess," Knight said.

"Okay, Daddy."

While our men and kids took care of the chores, we went about solving the problems of the world…or at least the get together happening in less than a week.

"Hawk and Payton are taking care of collecting and cataloguing the toys," Kim said. "I think Ace and Cassidy are collecting from the drops in Portland, and Hatch and Maisie are taking care of Vancouver."

"How many drops do we have now?" I asked.

"Ten."

"That's awesome." I smiled. "Darien got busy."

Kim chuckled. "She sure did. She got Melody Morgan involved, which means Mack had more to do."

Darien Reed was married to Mack, and a

very successful author. In fact, her multi-million selling romance novels were currently being turned into movies with the hottest actress, Melody Morgan, as its star.

I sipped my water. "Don't feel sorry for Mack, he loves every second of it."

"This is true."

"We're gonna get out of your hair," Knight said, handing Kim her jacket. "Ace and I'll be by after lunch tomorrow to grab everything and take it down to the compound."

I smiled up at him. "Thanks, buddy."

"No problem." He leaned down and kissed my cheek, then rubbed my belly gently, before helping his girls with their jackets and ushering his family out the front door.

"Anyone have homework?" Austin asked.

"No," both my kids answered.

"Okay, go shower and get ready for bed."

Once Cash and Archer left us, Austin sat on the sofa and set his beer on the coffee table. "How are my girls?"

I rolled my head to smile at him. "We're good, honey."

"Yeah?"

I nodded. "So good, I kinda wanna do dirty

stuff to you."

He laughed, but his eyes got soft as he leaned over and kissed me gently. "As soon as the boys are in for the night, I'll let you."

I licked my lips in anticipation. I loved this pregnancy. Mostly because I was horny all the time. Maybe it was because I was having a girl this time. With Cash and Archer, I was sick a lot and it took a while for me to feel normal. Now, however, I couldn't keep my hands off my husband and Austin was way into it.

Truth be told, he was always way into it, pregnancy or not.

Austin turned on the television for me, and as he went through the bedtime ritual with the boys, I found myself in and out of wakefulness for the next hour or so.

A gentle kiss woke me and I smiled up at my man. "Hey."

"Hey, baby. Let's get you into bed."

I shivered. "Yes, please."

"To sleep." He held his hands out and I let him pull me up.

"Hell, no. You promised."

"Did I?"

I leaned forward and ran my tongue over his

bottom lip. "You absolutely did."

He stroked my cheek. "You sure?"

"Ohmigod, Booker, get your sexy ass in the bedroom and get naked."

He chuckled. "Usin' my club name...you must be serious."

"I'm horny, so yes, I'm very serious."

He grinned, taking my hand and leading me to our bedroom. Once he locked us in, his mouth was on mine and he was removing our clothes. I loved how he could undress me in ten seconds or less (we'd timed it once), and then it was all about me and what I wanted.

"On your back," I said, and Austin stretched out on the bed.

"You gonna let me taste you?"

I smiled. "Of course I'm gonna let you taste me. I'm not a monster."

He chuckled and pointed to the headboard. "Assume the position, baby."

I crawled onto the bed and anchored myself to the headboard, while Austin slid his face between my legs, raising his head to run his tongue over my clit.

I shivered as my body to responded to him, like it always did. As he focused on sucking my clit, he slid two fingers inside of me and I dropped my head back as he played my pussy like an electric guitar. God, what this man could do to me, even after all these years.

My walls contracted around his fingers and then he was guiding me onto his cock and I was riding him while his thumb connected with my clit again.

"Austin," I breathed out.

"Hold it, baby," he begged.

It had always been difficult for me to keep my orgasms at bay, but over the past few months, it became virtually impossible. Austin knew this.

"Get there, honey," I ordered.

He gripped my hips and slammed up into me again and again, then finally, he grunted out, "Now, baby," and I came, settling my hands on his chest and smiling as we caught our breath.

"Fuck, I love you," he rasped.

"Back atya," I said, and climbed off of him, heading to the bathroom, sitting on the edge of the tub and settling my hands on my belly.

He followed. "What's wrong?"

I took a slow, deep breath. "Just had a little cramp."

He hunkered down in front of me. "No more sex."

I gasped. "Um, no, you don't get to arbitrarily make that decision."

"Dani, you're barely a month away from having our baby girl. I will not put you in jeopardy."

"But I can't go all that time without sex, Austin."

He sighed. "You just want me for my body."

"Well, this is true, but you knew that going into this partnership."

He chuckled. "I'm gonna get you some Tylenol, then bed for you."

I kissed him quickly. "I can live with that."

He grinned and after helping me into bed, he held me close and whispered to our baby until I fell asleep.

TWO

HAWK & PAYTON

*Payton*

"I GOT IT," Lily called out after the doorbell pealed.

"*I* will get it," Hawk growled. "Dad!"

"Baby girl, get your ass away from that door."

"It's Maverick."

"And I'm gonna answer it."

I rolled my eyes. Lily was almost seventeen and had been in love with Maverick Quinn since she was five (and he with her), but Hawk had a rule (one of many), and that was that he answered the door after six p.m. No exceptions.

"Ohmigod," she said with a groan.

"Go help your mom in the kitchen."

The doorbell pealed again, and Lily and Hawk argued for few more seconds before my girl stomped into the kitchen. "I think Dad's on his period."

I chuckled. "He just wants a couple of minutes with Maverick."

"Well, that sounds ominous."

I handed her a knife and nodded to the veggies. "Chop."

"I don't think you should be handing me a knife, Mom. My man isn't in front of me in one piece yet, and Dad's the reason he isn't."

Our heads turned at the sound of Maverick and Hawk laughing, so I once again nodded to the veggies. "I think you're good."

She sighed, but started to chop just as her brothers walked in. Hunter snagged a piece of carrot from Lily's pile and popped it into his mouth.

"Why's Dad grillin' Mav?" Case asked.

Case wasn't really Case. He was Lincoln, but when he was little, he was extremely bossy and was always getting on everyone's case, so we'd called him "Case," and it had stuck. Now, no one ever called him Lincoln, and it kind of made me sad at times, but it was what it was.

Lily set the knife down. "He's grilling him?"

Before Lily could slide off her barstool, Hawk and Maverick walked in and Maverick seemed perfectly fine.

"Hey, Lil," Maverick said, kissing her cheek. I noticed he kept PDAs to a minimum when everyone was around. That would be Cassidy's influence, because our men had no problem showing us how much they adored us...in public or private...and whenever the hell they wanted.

She beamed up at him. "Hi."

"You ready?" he asked.

"Yep."

"Did you drop everything off at the compound?" I asked Maverick.

"Yeah," he said. "Prez wasn't expectin' so many toys. They're planning on using one of the bunk rooms to store everything, but for now, it's all safe in the truck."

"That's great," I said. "Maisie said we have twice as many donations as last year."

"Three times," Maverick countered. "As of tonight."

"Even better."

"We also got Hatch's present hauled and hidden," Maverick said.

"What is it?" Lily asked.

"Secret," he said, but I had a feeling she'd get it out of him later.

I grinned, rinsing potatoes in the sink. I knew what it was, but Maisie had sworn me to secrecy, and telling any of my kids would not be a good way to keep that promise.

"We better go," Maverick said.

I set the spud in the bowl and faced them. "You guys have fun tonight."

"You drive like you're old and careful," Hawk said to Maverick.

Maverick smiled, wrapping his arm around

Lily. "Precious cargo, Hawk. Not lettin' anything happen to her."

"Okay, honey, I think you can release the tether, huh?" I challenged.

Hawk nodded. "You guys have fun."

In pure Lily fashion, she got the hell out of the house before her father could change his mind, and I grinned at him, kissing him quickly before ordering Hunter to take over Lily's chopping.

"Case, I'm gonna have you peel," I said.

"It's all good." Case shoved his face in the fridge and grabbed a rootbeer. "Want one, Hunt?"

"Nah, I'm good, thanks."

Case opened his pop and grabbed a peeler while I headed to the stove. My man closed the distance between us and wrapped his arms around me from behind, kissing my neck and whispering, "You wearin' anything under that?"

I shook my head and shivered, leaning back against him. I was wearing a long skirt (sans panties, which my man loved), and a V-neck T-shirt.

"You wet?" he asked, for my ears only.

I nodded. He did shit like this to me all the

time. It didn't matter who was around, he'd get me so fucking hot, I'd nearly implode on the spot. How he did it without anyone else hearing, I had no idea...but he was the master.

"Gonna take care of that in a minute, baby," he promised.

I swallowed and closed my eyes in anticipation. "I'd appreciate that, handsome."

He patted my hips and turned away from me, chatting with our kids like it was any normal day, while I stood at the stove and squeezed my thighs together.

Once our kids were done with their food prep, they decided to head up to the game room for a bit.

"Dinner in an hour," I called as they ran upstairs.

I heard their favorite video game start and Hawk bellowed, "Door."

The house grew quiet again and I wasn't surprised to find Hawk directly behind me. "Brace, Pay."

I leaned against the island and braced as he lifted my skirt from behind and slid his hand between my legs. "Spread."

I spread. "Alex, the boys—"

"Are busy." Two fingers slipped inside of me. "Soaked, baby."

I licked my lips and nodded.

"Spread more."

I did and was rewarded by his hand slapping against my pussy.

"Alex," I breathed out.

Before I could say anything else, my skirt was dropped, but Hawk stayed behind me.

"Mom?" Case called.

Ohmigod, how the fuck my husband knew we were going to be interrupted boggled my mind.

"Yeah, bud?"

"Oh, wait, never mind!" he called again. "Found it."

Hawk's hand slid between my legs again and he leaned close. "Payton, you're closed up. Fuckin' spread those legs."

I did as he ordered, my body primed for him. I heard his zipper open, then his dick was inside me and I was biting the inside of my cheek to keep from crying out.

"Not a sound," he rasped as he slammed into me from behind.

My nipples were hard enough to cut glass,

but I knew he'd do nothing to relieve that pressure. This was his way. His torture. His glorious, glorious torture.

He'd fuck me in public, then make love to me in private later, but I'd have to wait for him to take his time. This was our foreplay and it was exciting as hell.

"Come," he whispered, and I did. Ohmigod, how I did.

He rezipped his jeans, and got a kitchen towel wet before slipping it between my legs and cleaning me up. After slapping my ass, he threw the towel in the laundry room which was right off the kitchen.

"Can't wait to fuck your tits later," he said, kissing me deeply. He tugged one of my bra cups down and rolled a nipple between his fingers before righting my clothing with a grin. "Gonna fuck them hard."

I stroked his beard. "Can't wait, handsome."

"Can't huh?"

"Not happily, no."

He chuckled, raising my skirt (this time from the front) and slipping his hand between my legs again. "You need a little more relief?"

I nodded as I swallowed. "Please."

His thumb went straight to my clit, while three fingers pushed inside of me. I gripped his shoulders for balance and leaned into his hand. Hawk wrapped his free arm around my waist to anchor me to him as his fingers fucked me 'til I exploded.

In the middle of our kitchen.

It was *awesome.*

"I'm gonna let you feel that for a bit," Hawk said, kissing me again as he ran his hand through my wetness. "I'll lick you clean later."

I squeezed my legs closed. "Ohmigod, Alex. You're impossible."

He chuckled. "Just gave you two orgasms in the middle of the kitchen. I'm pretty sure I could fuck with your tits right now and give you another one, so impossible isn't the word that comes to mind, but okay, baby. Impossible it is."

I rolled my eyes.

"Love you," he whispered, kissing me again.

"Love you too," I rasped, leaning close. "Are you feeling better about Maverick and Lily officially dating?"

"No."

"Honey, he adores her. You know he'll take

care of her."

"She's my baby girl, Pay. I get it, but you're gonna need to give me a little while to get used to it."

I didn't point out that they'd been inseparable for more than ten years and that this stage in their relationship was inevitable. If Maverick was anything like his father, he'd already made Lily his in every way imaginable. I was actually okay with that, because I knew he was hers and had been forever.

"I can give you that, Alex."

Hawk wrapped his arms around me and held me for a few precious moments, then we went about finishing dinner.

THREE

## ACE & CASSIDY

*Cassidy*

**I** ARRIVED HOME before my family, so I dumped my dance bag in the laundry room and headed to my shower. Ace and the kids were at the compound decorating, blissfully giving me a night off. Considering I'd been there all week, I was *wiped*. On top of the party plans, I still had my normal schedule of dance classes, although, today was my last one for the season, so I had the next three weeks off.

As the water flowed over me, easing the pain in my muscles, I did a mental checklist of everything we still needed to do. I had been doing this every night for a week and I was grumpy. I shouldn't be. I loved every second, but I'd barely seen my husband, and I missed him.

"I love it when you're all wet."

I let out a squeal as I jumped, spinning to glare at my man through the fogged-up glass. *"Carter!"*

He chuckled. "Did I scare you, baby?"

"I swear to God, you are not funny."

"You swear to God I'm not funny?" he murmured as he stripped. "Can you do that? I mean, is that a thing?"

I pushed my wet hair away from my face and shook my head. "You're—"

"Not funny," he finished. "I know."

Sliding the door open, he stepped inside, and my heart raced at his beauty. God, I could not get enough of looking at him. Or touching him. He was tall and built, all sinew and muscle like he'd been formed from granite. Over ten years of marriage and this man still brought me to my knees.

Like now.

Wrapping my hand around his already rock-hard cock, I licked the drop of pre-cum off the tip, then ran my tongue up the base. "God, I've missed you."

He chuckled, his hand going to my head. "Apparently."

I looked up at him. "Are you going to let me finish?"

"Really want my cock inside your cunt, so probably not." He stroked my cheek. "But if you want me to lead you to believe otherwise for a minute, I'll do it."

I sighed and rose to my feet, sliding my hands up his chest. "How long do we have?"

"All night. Dropped the truck off at the compound, hid Hatch's gift from Maisie, Tillie's at Knight's, Liam's at Booker's, and Maverick's out with Lily."

I let out a quiet squeak and wrapped my arms around him. "Sixteen."

"Sixteen?"

"Orgasms. I want. I need."

He dropped his head back and laughed before cupping my cheeks and kissing me gently. "Challenge accepted."

Lifting me so I could wrap my legs around his waist, he guided himself inside of me, then anchored me to the shower wall.

"Fuck, you're soaked," he rasped, rolling a nipple between his fingers.

"As soon as you said we had all night, it was a flood."

He growled, kissing me deeply and slamming me into me as his tongue slid against mine. Even though I no longer danced for a professional company, ballet was still my life and I taught multiple times a week. This made me strong.

This fact made my man crazy, and it made him crazy because he could pretty much put me wherever he wanted me, and my body was limber enough to comply.

Ace was tall…I was small. It was a perfect match, and every time we made love, he worshiped me. Honestly, he worshiped me even when we weren't naked, and I adored him.

Keeping me tight to his body, he flipped off the water and gingerly carried me out of the bathroom and settled me on our mattress.

"Our sheets'll be soaked," I objected.

"Don't give a fuck," he said, and lifted my hips so he could bury himself deeper.

"That's because you don't have to sleep in the wet—oh!" I lost all coherent thought when he shifted, and his cock hit *the* spot. "*Ace.*"

"What were you sayin'?"

"Nothing. I was saying nothing," I panted out.

He hovered above me, then set one hand on the bed beside me and slid one to my clit, pressing his finger against it as he pushed inside of me again. "Still nothin'?"

I gripped his arm and lifted my hips. "Harder."

He stood up again and grinned down at me. "Legs up, baby."

I slid my legs from around his waist and anchored my ankles to his shoulders, and he pulled my body even closer to his.

Carter slammed into me once, holding my thighs steady and then he began to move, surging in and out of me faster and faster. I screamed his name as I came around him, but he wasn't done, and he ran a finger over my clit, building me up again.

"Grab your tits, baby."

I kneaded my breasts, rolling the nipples between my fingers and panting as another orgasm built.

"I'm close," I rasped.

"Come, baby," he demanded, and I exploded again.

I didn't have time to revel in the afterglow, as I was flipped onto my stomach and my ass was pulled up into the air. Carter's hand whispered over my back, then he settled his palm on my hip and leaned over me slightly. "That's two."

I shivered. My man was nothing if he wasn't a keeper of his word. And when he said he'd give me sixteen orgasms, he wouldn't stop until he gave me sixteen orgasms.

Sliding into me again, slowly, tortuously, he gripped my hips and pulled me back against him, but he didn't move. I wiggled in frustration, earning me a slap on my right butt cheek. "Carter," I growled.

"You're always in such a rush, Cass," he accused, burying himself deeper. "We've got all night."

"But I don't want to wait all night. I want all sixteen right now!"

He chuckled, sliding his hand between my legs. "Okay, baby. I've got you, but you better brace."

I braced and was rewarded with him slamming into me from behind as he worked my clit with his hand and I nearly fell over as an orgasm ripped through me faster than I anticipated. Carter wasn't far behind and we fell onto the mattress and he held me close as we caught our breath.

"That's what I'm talking about," I said, rolling to face him.

He chuckled, pushing my hair gently from my face, then stroking my cheek. "Do you know how much I love you?"

I turned my head so I could kiss his palm. "Yes. Because I love you just as much."

He grinned, tugging my head forward to kiss him...just as his phone buzzed on the night--stand.

"No, no, no, no!" I ground out, reaching for his arm. "Do not answer that."

He ignored me. "Ace," he said, then sat up. "What the fuck?"

"No, not what the fuck!" I snapped, covering my face with my hands. "What the fuck is never good for me. What the fuck is interrupting the *actual* fuck."

"When? Yeah? What did the cameras pick up? What do you mean, nothing?" He shot off the bed and headed into the bathroom. "Then you better call Booker and find out why that camera isn't workin'. God damn it, Flea, rally the fuckin' troops, whatever, but we have to find that truck. Just keep Hatch out of it for the moment. He finds his surprise from Maisie, she'll kill us."

I sat up. *Shit, this is bad.*

Ace walked back into the bedroom, jeans on and I shook my head. "Really?"

"Gotta go, baby. Someone stole the truck."

I gasped. "The Christmas truck?"

"No, the garbage truck."

"Oh, don't you dare give me that tone. It

could have been one of the tow trucks or something."

He sighed, dragging on a T-shirt. "Sorry, baby. Just a little pissed right now, but not at you."

I crawled to the edge of the bed and reached for him. "Can't someone else take care of it? You need a night off."

He slid his hands to my neck and stroked my pulse. "No one's gettin' a night off tonight, Cass. We have to find that truck or we won't have a party on Saturday."

"Who would steal a truck filled with kids' Christmas gifts?"

"An asshole, obviously," he said. "But the fucker messed with the wrong people."

I gripped his shirt. "Yes, he did, but please don't kill him…or them…or whomever. I really don't want you in jail on Christmas."

He smiled, kissing me gently. "We'll be careful."

Then he was gone. I groaned and fell back on the bed…straight into the wet spot. "Damn it!"

Since I had nothing better to do, I stripped the bed and grabbed dry sheets.

*  *  *

*Ace*

I hated leavin' Cassidy in our bed, especially when she was naked and frustrated, but if we didn't find the missing Christmas truck, there'd be no presents for some very deserving kids.

Walking into the compound, I found Booker in his office, his fingers flying over the keyboard, and I deduced he was doin' his voodoo computer thing. "You find anything?"

Booker glanced up and shook his head. "We have several iPads inside and I'm tryin' to activate the finders app. Just gotta find one that's on."

I glanced down at the list. There were more than "several" on it, so I knew this was gonna take a while.

FOUR

MACK & DARIEN

*Darien*

**I**CLOSED MY laptop at the sound of my husband letting out a series of very loud expletives and headed into the kitchen. "*What* is going on?"

Mack turned off the stove and slid his cell phone in his pocket. "Some asshole stole the truck."

"The truck, truck?"

Mack nodded.

"From the compound?"

"Yeah," he breathed out. "Apparently the camera that was supposed to be on it has been down for two days. Booker's got one on order, but it's late."

"Daddy?" Harper padded into the kitchen, rubbing her eyes. "Why are you yelling?"

He hunkered down in front of her. "Sorry, baby, I didn't mean to wake you. Everything's okay. Just something with work."

Harper patted his face, then hugged him. "It's okay. You'll work it out."

He stood back up with her in his arms kissed her cheek. "You're right. It'll all be fine. Come on, I'll tuck you back in."

We had two girls. Harper, ten, and Ryan, eight. I found it ironic that the biggest playboy on the planet ended up making girls, and now he'd have to deal with men like him when they got to dating age. He, on the other hand, couldn't have been happier. He was a great dad and I knew our girls would grow up to find men who cherished them the way their daddy did.

While Mack put Harper back to bed, I checked on Ryan who was sound asleep and probably wouldn't have woken up even if a gun had gone off. I headed back to the kitchen and peered into the pot on the stove.

"Pasta," he said, wrapping his arms around me from behind. "I was hungry."

"Apparently." I turned to face him, looping my arms around his neck.

"Did you get your wordcount in?"

"I overachieved and wrote an extra thousand," I said. "Do you need to go to the compound?"

"Not yet. Ace and Booker are over there now. Why?"

I licked my lips. "Because I just wrote the dirtiest sex scene to date, and it kind of got me super hot."

I was a romance author and Logan "Mack" Reed was my muse.

He chuckled, sliding his hands under my T-shirt. "Yeah?"

"Yeah."

"How hot?"

"Nipple clamp hot."

He tugged my bra down and ran his thumbs over my already hard nipples. "Love it when you say 'toys.'"

I giggled. "I know you do."

"I think the pasta can wait."

"I think it can too." I grabbed his hand and led him into our bedroom. Luckily, our master suite was on the opposite side of the house from the kids, so noise wasn't a problem.

Mack locked the door behind us heading straight for the closet and the locked box with our toys while I got naked. With a very inquisitive daughter, we'd learned pretty quickly (when she walked out of our bedroom holding my bright pink vibrator, and asking if she could play with the 'magic fairy wand') to lock things up.

Mack pulled a set of clamps out of the box and I bit my lip as he attached one, then the other. Instead of letting the chain fall in front, he wrapped it around the back of my neck, which pulled my nipples up and I squirmed at the sensation.

"Too tight?" he asked.

I shook my head. "Tighter," I rasped.

He twisted the tightener and I dropped my head back with a sigh. He slid his hand between my legs and ran a finger through my wetness.

"Soaked," he whispered.

I met his eyes. "Did I mention the scene was super hot?"

"On your knees, Dare."

I climbed onto the bed and assumed the position, while Mack took his clothes off and situated himself behind me. I glanced at him just as his head disappeared between my legs and his tongue ran through my folds. I ground down against his face and he continued his feast until he brought me to the brink…then stopped. "*Logan*," I growled.

He chuckled, kneeling behind me again and sliding into me. I sighed and dropped my head back slightly which tugged on my clamps, sending a glorious sensation all the way to my clit. "Fuck, you feel amazing," Mack rasped.

He leaned over me, his hand slipping between my legs and his fingers going to my clit, while he wrapped his other hand around my chain.

"Oh god," I whispered.

Then he moved. Slowly at first, before slamming into me as he fingered my clit and tugged on the chain. I was swamped with…well, everything.

"Logan," I rasped.

"Come, baby."

I did, but he wasn't done, and as he thrust harder, he built me up again. He yanked the chain so hard, one clamp popped off, but even that was a delicious sensation. The sudden tug sent a shockwave to my pussy and I cried out as another orgasm washed over me.

Mack's cock pulsed inside of me and we fell onto the mattress in a gentle heap of body parts. He wrapped his arms around me and pulled me close, gently releasing the clamp that was still attached, before kissing my shoulder. "It just gets better."

I nodded, linking my fingers with his and pulling our hands up to my mouth. "So so good."

Releasing his fingers from mine, he moved his hand between my legs and palmed my mound. "You sure you don't wanna try for a boy?"

I closed my eyes and smiled. We'd had this

conversation a million times before. One finger slipped inside of me. "Do you remember how much you loved to be fucked when you were pregnant?"

"I do." I gasped as another finger slid inside and his thumb pressed against my clit. "But I also remember how tired I was afterwards and how hard it was to find that mojo again. And how I still haven't lost my Ryan weight."

"Baby, you could gain—"

"A hundred pounds, I know," I finished.

His cock replaced his fingers, but his thumb stayed pressed against my clit. "How great would a boy be, though?"

"I'll think about it," I said. It was the same thing I said every time. Truth be told, I wasn't opposed to another child, but we were also in such a good place that I didn't want to upset the apple cart, so to speak.

"You know I'll worship at your feet."

"Honey, you always worship at my feet..." His thumb pressed harder on my clit and I whimpered with need.

"We need a boy."

"With the track record of your sperm, though, we'd probably get another girl."

Applying pressure to my clit again, he whispered, "I'm good with another girl, too, Dare."

I pulled away from his hand and shifted to face him, pushing him on his back and straddling him. "Why do you pull all the manipulation tactics when you're doing shit to my pussy?"

His beautiful face broke out into a grin. "Because you'll agree to almost anything when I'm doing shit to your pussy."

"Newsflash: I agree to almost anything when it comes to you."

His hand went back to my clit and I pressed down against it as his fingers slid inside again. I let him have his way with my pussy for a few minutes, before guiding his cock back inside of me, and raising and lowering myself as I anchored myself to his chest. He raised his knees and propelled me forward slightly, which gave him better access to me. I grinned, leaning down to run my tongue over the Dogs of Fire logo on his pec, then switching to do the same to the tattoo over his heart. A heart-shaped Celtic knot with all of his girls' names inked permanently on his skin.

I sat up and his hands palmed my breasts

while he raised his hips to slam up into me while I gripped his wrists for balance. Before I could get into any kind of groove, however, I found myself on my back and Mack burying himself deeper and deeper as I wrapped my legs around his waist. He stroked my neck as he kissed me gently, our tongues mimicking the movements of our bodies.

"Don't come," he growled, obviously feeling my body about ready to explode.

"You need to get there, honey," I countered, scraping a nail down his nipple. It didn't take long before he let out a grunt, so I let myself join him in climax.

He kissed me again before slipping out of me and heading to the bathroom. He didn't linger and joined me back on the bed, settling a warm washcloth between my legs.

Stretching out on his back, he pulled me over his chest and I tucked my face into his neck and snuggled close. "It's very possible you put a baby in me right then," I said.

Mack chuckled. "One can hope."

"I really will think about it, honey."

He cupped my cheek and tipped my chin up to meet his eyes. "No pressure. We do this, we do this together. That won't ever change."

I smiled. "I know, honey. I hear you."

"You wanna drink some wine and make-out in front of the TV?"

"Hells, yeah I do," I said, and sat up.

Mack grinned and we got dressed in our pajamas. Since we were both now starving, he resurrected his pasta concoction, and after we ate, we snuggled up on the sofa.

FIVE

KNIGHT & KIM

*Kim*

**K**NIGHT WALKED INTO the house and slammed the door. I turned off the kitchen faucet and grabbed a towel, meeting him in the foyer. "Still no luck?"

He kicked off his boots and shook his head. "Booker's been workin' on it for hours, but there are close to a hundred iPads he has to go through and so far, none of them are on."

I bit my lip. "That sucks...but can I just say, a hundred iPads? That's so incredibly awesome. People really stepped up this year."

He sighed. "Yeah, sugar, it's awesome. Unless the asshole who stole the truck is already selling them and makin' a mint."

Dropping the towel on the console, I slid my hands around his waist. "You guys'll find the truck, honey. I'm confident of it. If not, we'll still have a great party because you and I'll cover the cost of new toys."

He pulled me close. "Don't wanna have to do that, Kim."

"I know. Me neither. But it's nice to know we can."

"Daddy!" Cambry squealed, making a run for us. Jagger wasn't far behind, and the four of us ended up in a snuggle pile on the floor with Knight taking most of the weight. Lucky for us, my man was big and strong.

"Okay, monkeys, dinner's almost ready," I said. "Go wash up."

The kids climbed off their dad and made a run for the downstairs bathroom, while Knight helped me up, pushing me against the foyer wall and kissing me deeply. I wove my fingers into his hair and tugged gently.

"Why do you rile me up when we can't do anything about it?" I complained.

His hand cupped my breast. "Just primin' the pump, sugar. Gonna turn the valve into the fully open position later."

I giggled. "Yeah, that 'valve' will definitely be open."

He gave me a sexy grin. "I know it will."

"Ew, gross," Jagger said. "Dad's kissin' Mama again."

Cambry giggled. "Why are you always kissing?"

Knight smiled at me. "It's one of the ways I show Mom how much I love her."

I beamed up at him, sliding my hand to his waist again and giving him a gentle squeeze.

"If Sam Wallers kisses me, does that mean he loves me?" she asked, and the look on my husband's face both terrified and amused me.

He hunkered his big body down in front of Cambry and asked, "Did Sam Wallers kiss you?"

She shook her head. "He said he loves me, and he puckered his lips, but Cash walked over to me before he could."

I bit my lip. Dani's kid was super protective of Cambry, and I loved that they were in the same private school.

Knight settled his hands on Cambry's arms. "No boy should be kissin' you, Cambry. If a boy likes you, he better show you some respect and be your friend. If he wants to kiss you, you tell him your daddy'll kill him if he does."

"Okay, maybe not say that," I countered. "But it's real important that you respect yourself, sweet girl, and letting boys kiss you just because they say they love you, isn't how you do it."

"You need to make 'em sweat a little," Knight said.

Cambry smiled. "You're funny, Daddy. Sweating's gross."

"So is kissing."

She dropped her head back with a dramatic eye roll and groaned. "*Fine.*"

"Cambry, you handle drinks tonight, okay?" I said. "Jagger, knives and forks."

"Okay, Mom," Jag said.

"We're gonna decorate the tree after dinner."

"Yay!" Jagger said, pumping his fist in the air before heading out of the foyer.

Knight kissed Cambry's forehead and she skipped off to the kitchen. He rose to his feet and faced me with a frown. "Who the fuck is this Sam kid?"

"First I've heard," I said. "I'll talk to Dani about it tomorrow. Maybe Cash said something."

Knight let out a quiet growl. "Fuckin' hate dicks."

I chuckled. "I get it, honey. We have a long time before we have to worry about actual dicks, though. It's all gonna be okay."

He kissed me gently, then we went about serving dinner.

After the tree was decorated, hot cocoa was consumed, and our kids were tucked in bed, I followed Knight to our bedroom where he proceeded to practically rip my clothes from my body. "Still primed, sugar?"

I nodded.

"Shower," he demanded, and I stalked there and flipped on the water.

Kissing me, he lifted me inside the gigantic, tiled space (with six shower heads) and gently pushed me up against the wall. As I tilted my head out of the water, Knight put his lips against my neck and slid his hand between my legs. He ran his fingers across my wet folds, and his dick pulsed against my hip.

My hips arched into his hand. "Fuck me."

"How hard?" he asked, sliding one finger through my wetness.

I shivered and pushed against his hand. "Hard."

He grinned as he shoved a finger inside me and bit my neck.

"Aidan," I growled. "I want your cock."

He stroked me a few times, then pulled his fingers out and demanded, "Hands on the wall."

I turned and slapped my palms against the tile.

He grabbed my hips as I arched my ass up. But he still didn't give me his cock. Instead, his knees hit the floor and he ran a tongue over my wetness. "Love your cunt, sugar."

"*Ohmigod, ohmigod,*" I panted out.

He sank two fingers back inside me and took my clit between his teeth.

My body shuddered as he rotated his fingers and rubbed deep inside, hitting my G-spot as he sucked my clit. I whimpered as my climax built, but then he backed off my pussy and rose to his feet.

"Knight," I snapped.

"Patience, sugar."

"Fuck patience," I ground out, and I was rewarded with his cock. He buried himself to the hilt and slid a hand between my legs again to finger my clit.

"Love your tight cunt, Kim."

I dropped my head to the tile and tried not to pass out from the sensations swamping me.

Palming one nipple, he twisted the other, as he reared back and slid into me one slow, torturous inch at a time. I could feel my pussy pulsing and I took one hand off the wall and slid it to my clit. While he focused on my tits and I focused on my clit, he pulled almost all the way out again, then drove back into me all at once.

I sucked a breath through my teeth and pushed my ass against him. Rearing back, he slammed into me again, grabbing a handful of my hair and tugging my head back so he could reach my mouth with his.

His tongue connected with mine as he buried his dick inside of me again, then he released my hair and focused on fucking me senseless.

"Knight," I rasped. "I can't—"

"Now, sugar."

Dropping my head back against his shoulder, I exploded and he wasn't far behind me, his cock pulsing as we came together.

"Holy shit," I breathed out. "Amazing."

He chuckled, kissing the sensitive spot behind my ear before turning me to face him and cupping my cheeks. "Love you, Kim."

"I love you, too, honey."

He kissed me again, then we finished our shower and headed to bed.

SIX

## HATCH & MAISIE

*Maisie*

*Thirty-six hours later…*

"**C**ONNOR WALLACE, I will hurt you," I threatened from my place between the wall and one of our high-backed chairs. The Christmas tree was to the right of me, so I didn't really have much of an escape route.

His gorgeous, bearded face lit up with a cheeky grin. "Not afraid of you, Sunshine, now come out of there."

"Not until you promise you won't make me pee."

He laughed. "Not promisin' you shit."

I had a secret, and Hatch wanted to know what it was, but I was a vault. However, he thought tickling the information out of me would be a good idea…this meant I was running around the house like a mad woman, trying to keep something between us at all times.

"She's not going to tell you anything, Sid," Poppy taunted as she held our two-year-old, Jamie's, hand and kept him out of the fray.

Flash, on the other hand, was trying to help out his dad in catching me. He was almost four and a total and complete carbon copy of Hatch. "Parker," I warned as he tried to drag me from my hiding place.

He just squealed with laughter.

"Flash, come on outta there," Hatch said. "This is between your mom and me."

We called him Flash because he was ridiculously quick…to get into trouble or out of my line of sight.

"Come with me, little brother," Poppy said, holding her free hand out to him. "We'll watch the show from here."

Flash rushed to her and I focused back on my husband. "I'm not telling you anything, darling, so there's no point in trying to torture me."

"Oh, the torture part's just for me."

I bit my lip as desire rushed my nether regions. Hatch always said he loved to see me laugh because I had a similar look on my face when I came, and he only ever wanted to see me happy or climaxing. He might be in the mood to torture me one way right now, but the promise of a different kind of torture later made me shiver in anticipation.

"I can see you like that," he murmured.

"You know I do."

"Okay, I'm out," Poppy said, and grabbed Flash's hand again. "Mummy and Daddy are about to kiss, so why don't we go get a snack?"

I giggled as my very wise daughter guided her brothers toward the kitchen. My distraction had been a mistake, however, and I found my-self yanked gently from my hiding place and pulled up against the hard granite chest of my husband. I met his eyes and smiled. "Hi."

"Hey, Sunshine." He grinned. "You ready to talk?"

"Nope." I gave an extra pop sound to the P and then ran my fingers through his beard. "But I'll be happy to let you try again when we're na-ked and your face is between my legs."

His tongue slid along the seam of my lips and then he kissed me deeply, slipping one of his hands under my T-shirt and up my back.

"Hatch," I warned, even as my bra was un-hooked, and his hand moved to cup my breast.

"Yeah, sunshine?"

"The kids," I panted out as he palmed my al-ready rock-hard nipple.

"What about 'em?"

"They're—oh," I breathed out on a sigh as he slid his hand under the waistband of my yoga pants and between my legs.

"They're what, sunshine?"

He pulled his hand away from my body and I whimpered with need as he slid his fingers into his mouth and licked them clean. "Upstairs.

Now."

I didn't argue, and headed for the stairs.

"Poppy, watch your brothers for a bit. Gonna help your mom with something real quick."

"Okay, Sid."

God bless my daughter and her willingness to watch her brothers so my husband could drag me into our bedroom for a quick shag.

Walking into our room, I pulled off my shirt and bra, then rushed to remove the rest of my clothing. Hatch locked the door and grinned, pointing to the bed. "Assume the position, sunshine."

I giggled, stretching out on my back while I watched him strip. God, I'd never get enough of my man's body. He grinned, kneeling on the bed and crawling between my legs. He always started here…his mouth on my pussy…and I *loved* it.

Sliding his tongue through my folds, I wove my fingers into his hair and arched into his mouth. He slid two fingers inside of me and twisted them while he bit down gently on my clit and I nearly came apart, but I wanted to enjoy this…wanted it to last, so I stowed my orgasm and allowed his touch to consume me. I came apart, but didn't linger in the feeling, instead demanding my man lie on his back.

"Only if I get to taste you," he countered.

I smiled and straddled his face, before wrapping my fingers around his hardening length and taking it into my mouth. Hatch went to work on my pussy and I was having a hard time focusing on the beauty that was his dick while he sucked my clit.

"On your knees," he said.

I immediately went there. Hatch knelt behind me and guided himself inside of me and I dropped my head back at the sensation.

His palm connected with my bare bottom and I whimpered pushing my body back against him.

"Love how your body responds, sunshine." He slammed into me again, his palm slapping me a little harder this time and the sensation overtook everything.

God, it felt amazing, but when he slid one hand between my legs and fingered my clit, I came the second the palm of his other hand slapped against my bottom again, and I cried out his name as I buried my face in the mattress while he continued to thrust into me. As he came inside of me, he wrapped his arms around me, gently rolling us to the side so we were spooning, staying connected as he kissed the back of my neck...just as his phone buzzed on the nightstand.

"Do not answer that," I ordered.

He sighed. "All hands, baby. Need to be ready to go when they find the truck."

"But I wanted more," I grumbled as he answered his call.

"Hey, Book. Yeah? No shit? Okay, yeah, I'll meet you guys there." He hung up and slid off the bed.

"Did they find it?" I asked.

"Yeah, baby." He leaned down and kissed me quickly. "I'll text you when I know something."

He dressed quickly, and I was left somewhat unsatisfied in our bed. He'd make up for that later, I'd demand it, but I still hated that I had to prepare dinner while still horny.

I sighed and climbed out of bed, dressing quickly and heading downstairs to hang out with my children.

\* \* \*

*Hatch*

I pulled my truck up to the compound about twenty minutes later. I was glad there wasn't traffic from Vancouver into Cully, but I was still the last one to arrive, which surprised me a little. Several of us lived on the same street...our own commune, so to speak...so how the hell they got there before me was a mystery. Walking into the compound, I was met with my brothers flooding toward me.

"You're the last one," Booker said. "Let's roll."

I turned around and followed them outside again, Hawk and Ace climbin' into the cab of my truck, while the rest scattered. "Where are we goin'?" I asked.

"Beaverton," Hawk said.

"Shit, it's that close?"

"Yeah, man."

I followed Booker (who was on his bike), and the rest of the crew and we headed for the area that the iPad had pinged from. It took several minutes, but we finally located the big red truck in an alley, in one of the roughest parts of town.

Parking on the street, we pulled our guns out and approached the truck very carefully.

The alley was located directly behind an old brick building that had originally been a glass factory in the early nineteen-hundreds, but now served as one of the city's largest homeless shelters. The truck was tightly wedged between the alley walls, leaving only the slightest gap between its bright red doors and the exposed brick. I scratched my head, trying to figure out how the driver could have even gotten out of the cab. Once we reached the rear of the truck, Booker examined the lock on the back door.

"The lock's still intact," he said.

"Why the fuck do you think they left it here?" I asked.

Booker shook his head. "I dunno. Maybe whoever took it got spooked and dumped it, or maybe they chose this as a quiet place to stash it for a while."

"Quiet is right," Hawk agreed. "This place is a ghost town."

"That's good for us," Booker said. "The cops haven't seemed to notice this being here, so we can simply take it back without getting law enforcement or anyone else involved."

"Merry Christmas," I replied.

He smiled. "Ho, ho, ho."

"Now, how the fuck are we gonna get in the cab?" Knight asked.

"How did *they* get out?" Ace whispered.

"You're wondering that too, huh?" I asked.

"Sunroof?" Booker said.

Hawk piped up, "You don't s'pose they're still in there, do you?"

We all looked at each other and in unison responded, "Shit."

"Hatch, you and Hawk go around the block, to the other end of the alley and make your way back toward us," Booker said. "I'll boost Ace up to the top of the truck in case anyone tries to leave via the sunroof. Knight and I'll cover the rear in case this is all a trap."

"Got it," I said, and Hawk and I broke out in a slow jog around the block. The crisp night air felt good in my lungs, and it helped cool me from the burning surge of adrenaline. God knows who or what we'd find at the other end of the alley, but I tried to prepare myself for anything.

As we made our way down the alley, I could barely make out the truck's grill, reflected in what little light was being cast. I gripped my gun tightly, preparing myself physically and mentally for what I may be forced to do to defend myself. I sure hoped it wouldn't come down to anything drastic. Gunplay at Christmastime just didn't seem right.

"I can see Ace on the roof," Hawk said as we got closer.

I signaled to Ace who gave us a thumbs-up in response. We slowly approached the front of the truck and I tried to position myself to get a closer look into the cab. Given its height and precariously wedged position, this would prove difficult to do without detection. Should someone actually be in there, the last thing I wanted them to do was start blasting their way out of the cab, or take off down the alley with me on the hood or Hawk under the wheels.

I stood on some wooden pallets that were stacked to one side of the alley, peered inside the cab, but still couldn't see anyone inside. Just as I was about to hop down from my position, something caught my eye giving me pause. Located behind the truck's seats was a small sleeper compartment, big enough for one person to get some shut eye while out on the road. Although, I couldn't quite make out a figure, I could see what looked like a large red blanket wadded up on the twin bed. I pulled out my cell phone and turned on the flashlight to get a better look, just as the "blanket" began to move.

"There's someone inside," I whispered to Hawk as I ducked out of sight. I turned off the light, and returned the phone back to my pocket.

"What's the plan?" he whispered back.

"You cover me while I give this fucker a little wakeup call. Get ready to move back in case he's packing."

I gently and silently climbed onto the hood, and once in position tapped on the glass with the barrel of my gun.

The large red lump barely stirred. I tapped again, a little more vigorously but the truck's occupant remained still. I looked up at Ace who gave me a shrug. My eyes had now adjusted to darkness and I was able to make out more details within the tuck. I could clearly see an empty bottle of Jack Daniels on the floor, next to a string of wadded up Christmas lights.

I gave the window one more tap, and trying to remain as quiet as possible, but loud enough for the thief to hear me, said, "Wake up, fucker, we've got you surrounded." This finally got his attention. He shot out of bed, hitting his head squarely on the cab's ceiling, sending him straight back to the mattress, and wincing in pain.

"Put your hands where I can see 'em," I said a little louder.

"What the fuck, man? What the hell is going on here?" he asked as he sat up, clearly in a daze.

I could finally see the thief clearly, but could barely believe what I was seeing. Santa Claus had stolen our truck.

"Who is it?" Ace called down.

"You wouldn't believe me if I told you."

"Hey man, where am I?" Santa asked in a half lucid, gravelly tone.

"How about you just put your hands where I can see them and get the fuck out of the truck?" I said again.

"Truck? Why am I in a truck?" he asked while raising his black gloved hands.

"That's a great question, St. Nick."

He looked down at the full Santa suit he had

on and then back to me with a genuine expression of surprise. "Why am I in a truck, why am I dressed as Santa, and why the fuck are you pointing a gun at me? You a cop?" he asked.

"We can talk about all of this when you get out of our truck. Do you have a weapon in there?"

"A weapon? No man, I—" A wave of realization washed over Santa's face. "Oh shit, the kids."

"What kids? Are there children in there with you?" I asked, suddenly very concerned about what psycho Santa might be capable of. For all I knew, this drunken nut job had escaped from the looney bin.

"No, the kids at the shelter," he said.

"Look, man, you're not making any sense, and we just want our truck back. Why don't you come out of there now and we'll figure this out? How 'bout you slowly make your way to the driver's seat and open the door."

"How the hell am I gonna get outta here? I'm pretty jammed in."

With every passing moment, Santa seemed less and less like a dangerous criminal and more like a guy who wasn't quite sledding with all eight reindeer. I was guessing the empty pint bottle on the floor had much to do with that.

"Hey man, I'm sorry. I'm not even sure how I got here," he continued.

"You still have the keys?" I asked Santa, as Ace slid down the windshield to join me and Hawk, our guns still drawn.

"What the fuck?" Ace said as he spotted the cab's jolly occupant.

Santa reeled back and thrust his arms up higher.

"It's okay, I've got this, guys," I said before returning my attention back to Santa. "The keys? Do you still have them?"

Santa nodded. "Yeah, I think so, they should be in my pocket."

"Okay, I want you to *slowly* take the keys out and start up the truck. We've got guys behind you, so don't even think about doing anything stupid or I'll put a bullet through the windshield. I don't even care if it gets me on your naughty list."

Santa did as I asked, and I guided him down the alley until the truck reached a point where he could easily get out.

"Okay, kill the engine and slowly exit the cab

with your hands up," I called out, and as soon as he was out, I had him pinned against the side of the truck with his hands behind his back.

"Hey, c'mon, man, I ain't gonna hurt nobody," he said in a slight southern drawl.

"Please forgive me if I don't quite trust the guy that just boosted a truck full of toys," I said.

"Toys?" he replied. "Aw, shit. Oh, no," he said.

"Holy shit! You guys gotta see this!" I heard Knight yell from the rear of the truck.

"Come on," I said to Santa and we all moved to the back of the truck, which Knight and Booker had opened.

"We were gonna check to see if anything was missing, and it looks like we picked up a new donation instead," Knight said, smiling.

I looked inside and could see a 1994 Harley Road King, laying down, surrounded by brightly wrapped gifts and toys.

"My bike! Oh, shit, what have I done? I was just trying to help the kids at the shelter. What the hell have I done?" he asked, his large frame slumping to the ground with a thud.

I pulled his dirty fake beard down, revealing an only slightly less scruffy one, on a face that looked like it had seen better days.

I sighed. "Okay, man. We'll get you back to the compound and figure it out."

"He's not fuckin' comin' back to the compound," Ace growled.

"He's wasted, Ace. We need to sober him up and get some fuckin' answers. This guy's clearly no threat to us. Besides, he rides. What are we gonna do, take him to the cops?"

Ace studied me, then shook his head. "He'd better fuckin' have some answers."

I nodded and I helped Santa to his feet while Ace maneuvered the truck from between the buildings. While Ace took care of the truck, I loaded our new stray into my truck and we headed back to the compound.

SANTA CLAUS

## Hatch

**S**ANTA PASSED OUT in the truck on the way back, but he woke up pretty quickly when I pulled into the parking lot of the compound.

"We're here. Don't do anything stupid," I instructed.

"Where's *here*?" he asked.

He seemed a little more lucid and thanked me softly when I handed him a bottled water.

"You're at our compound. No one here's gonna hassle you if you co-operate, but you've gotta understand the situation we're in. You stole our truck, and more importantly, you stole from a bunch of kids at Christmas."

He looked up at me, "I know that, but I never—"

I interrupted, "We'll talk about it inside with the Prez."

He nodded.

"One more thing, there's no way I'm introducing you to everyone as Santa, so why don't you give me your name."

"Scott Bohman," he replied.

"Can't say I'm pleased to meet you just yet, but my name's Hatch. I'm the Sargent at Arms for the Dogs of Fire. Like I said, shoot strait with us, and we'll deal with you accordingly." I lowered my gaze and my tone. "Try to fuck with us…and we'll deal with you accordingly."

"I've been around," he replied.

"I have no trouble believing that whatsoever, Scott. Let's go." I lead him inside, where everyone had already gathered in the great room.

Booker had clearly filled Crow in on everything, and he sat with a scowl on his face.

"Crow, this is Scott Bohman, from..." I looked at him.

"Florida, um, Gainesville, Florida," he replied, extending a hand to Crow, who simply glared back.

"And what exactly brings you here to the Pacific Northwest? More specifically, what the fuck are you doing in my town, stealing my property?"

"I've got no excuse, sir, and I truly apologize. I don't drink...well, I haven't drank in a really long time...and I'm not really sure of all the details, but I think I was...trying to help."

Although Scott was big, and clearly looked like he could handle himself, he was as calm and gentle as I'd ever seen a person. You would never have guessed in a million years that this guy had boosted a truck in the middle of the night.

"How is stealing my truck helping me?" Crow demanded.

"Not you, so much as the kids back at the shelter where I'm staying."

"I think maybe we should get Scott here a seat and some coffee. Whatta ya say, Prez?" I asked.

"I swear, I don't mean any trouble to y'all and I'll figure out a way to make this up to you in any way I can. Everything's still in the truck," Scott said. "All of it. I promise."

"Take a seat. Someone get him some coffee and a coat that doesn't make me feel like sitting on this guy's lap," Crow called out, clearly relaxing a bit. "Who are you, Scott?"

"I'm just a guy riding across the country. Well, I guess I'm a guy who's *ridden* across the country now."

"You rode here from Florida?" Crow asked. "On a bike?"

Scott nodded. "I set off a year ago, and have sort of zig-zagged around the country. Working here and there, sleeping wherever I can. That sort of thing."

"By working, you mean boosting trucks and fencing the goods? Or do you mean specifically robbing children's charities?"

"I told you, I was blind drunk and stealing

your truck seemed like a good idea at the time."

"A good idea?" I challenged.

"I said it *seemed* like a good idea. Obviously, I was outta my fucking mind. Look, I've been staying at this shelter for about a week and it's filled with kids that aren't gonna see Jack Shit for Christmas, let alone Jack Frost. I was drinkin', feeling sorry for myself, and then I started feelin' sorry for all those little kids. The next thing I knew, I was in the suit and behind the wheel of the rig. I'm not even sure how I got into the alley."

"It's a miracle you didn't kill anybody," Crow said.

"I hadn't had a drink in over ten years before yesterday morning," Scott said with tears welling in his eyes as Booker handed him a cup of coffee, which he took and thanked him for. "But I drank until I couldn't see straight, and I can only see the rest in blurry snapshots. I remember a bell ringing and wrestling with Santa, then I remember pulling on a string of Christmas lights. I have a vague recollection of driving, then the next thing I knew, Hatch was tapping on the windshield."

"Why start up again yesterday?" Crow asked.

"I don't want to talk about that," Scott said, rising to his feet, the tone in his voice darkening instantly. My hand instinctively went to my sidearm and I unsnapped my holster. As harmless as he seemed, this guy was clearly far from stable.

Crow waved a hand. "It's okay, we're just talking here. Go ahead and sit back down or you'll make Hatch nervous."

Scott did as he was asked and continued, "I'm sorry, it's just...something I haven't talked about...with anyone."

"Look, man, you've clearly been through some shit, but you can't go around stealing just because you got loaded," I said.

"I wasn't stealing," he sighed. "I mean, yeah, obviously I stole your truck, but like I said, in my drunken mind, I was trying to play Santa to a bunch of needy kids, just like I used to." Scott's face fell. He looked like a shell of a man and my heart went out to him.

He continued, "You guys saw my bike. I've ridden with my friends back in Florida all my life. Never in a formal club or anything, but we had our guys, and every Christmas, we'd join in with a bunch of other local area bikers and do a big toy drive. I was at Duke's bar on Fifth and I saw y'all's rig pull up for a donation pick up. Something inside me snapped when I saw it was a club drive, so I followed you back here. I sat and watched, getting more and more drunk, until it got dark and the coast was clear. I remember the keys were in the truck and then it all gets real fuzzy."

"Ace, call Duke and ask him if he remembers anything from last night," Crow said.

"I swear I'm telling you guys the truth," Scott said.

"Maybe you *are* telling us the truth, but you aren't telling us the *whole* truth."

"What do you mean? I told you everything I can remember."

"Everything except for what you were running from in Florida, why you fell off the wagon after a ten-year ride, and what triggered a Florida Gator to put on the big red suit."

"I told you I don't want to talk about that," Scott replied.

"And I can't trust a man if I don't know his motivations, and if I can't trust you, I certainly can't just let you waltz outta here when I don't know what you're capable of."

"Come on, Crow, what's the guy gonna do, come back in April for our Easter baskets?" Booker asked. "Look at him."

"I *am* looking at Mr. Gator here, Booker, and he looks like trouble to me, and troubled people are dangerous. It's my job to protect this club from dangerous people."

"I'm not dangerous," Scott replied.

"What do you call getting loaded and getting behind the wheel of a stolen semi-truck?"

"Regrettable," Scott answered with zero self-pity in his tone. "Out of everything I've done, I regret that more than anything. Please believe me that it won't happen again."

"I don't believe you, because I don't know you. You won't even tell us what you're doing here, or why you've been hoboing across the country for a year. It's time to get the cops involved. If you don't want to talk to us, maybe you should talk to them," Crow said matter-of-factly.

Scott swiped a hand over his forehead. "I lost my wife and daughter. They were killed in a car accident exactly one year ago yesterday. I was married for twelve years. My daughter Caitlin was ten-years-old." He buried his face in his hands before composing himself and continuing, "I'm sorry, I don't talk about this, ever. I hit the road after the funeral and haven't been back home since. I left with nothin' but the clothes on my back and my ten-year coin in my pocket, and now I don't even have that."

"Jesus, brother, that's terrible," Crow said.

Ace came back into the room. "I just got off the phone with Duke and apparently someone stole the clothes, beard, and hat from the life-size animatronic Santa he puts by the front door every year, along with all the Christmas light's he'd just put up."

Crow looked up at our guest. "Alright, Gator, let's figure out what we're gonna do with you."

\* \* \*

*Maisie*

"What do you mean, he's still there?" I breathed out. "You're supposed to be keeping him away from the compound, not give him reasons to stick around."

"Babe, he's here. We got a situation, but I'm just givin' you a heads-up," Hawk said.

"Hawk," I said, very slowly. "Hatch cannot,

under any circumstances, go into the back of that shop."

"Maisie, we *know*. If I knew you were gonna bust my fuckin' balls, I woulda kept you in the dark. We're handlin' it."

I sighed. "Okay, Hawk. I appreciate that."

"Talk to you later."

He hung up and I made a plan, letting Poppy know I wouldn't be long (I hoped), and went to make sure my man didn't get nosy. As I drove into Cully, I had a moment of guilt, mostly because I had always promised Hatch I wouldn't drive down here alone, but desperate times and all that. I just hoped he wouldn't be too angry, especially when he saw what I was hiding.

I pulled into the compound without incident, made it through the first door, then the second, before stepping into the lobby where my arm was grabbed (gently) and I was pulled up against a very familiar body. "What the fuck are you doin' here, sunshine?" Hatch growled.

Okay, I think I may have made a rash choice.

"Told ya we had it handled, Maisie," Hawk ground out.

"I know…but…"

Hatch turned on his brother. "Are you tryin'

to tell me you're the reason my woman drove down here alone?"

"You wanna fill him in, Maisie?" Hawk challenged.

I grimaced.

"Come with me," Hatch growled and led me into the kids' playroom, slamming the door behind us. He crossed his arms and stood amongst a plastic kiddie oven, dollhouse, and building blocks, looking like he might kill someone. "Start talkin'."

I bit my lip. "I don't actually want to."

"What the fuck, Maisie?" he snapped.

"If I tell you why I'm here, I'll have to tell you what my surprise is," I revealed. "And I really don't want to do that."

He scowled. "My surprise is here?"

"Um, no?" I lied.

"What's the deal, Maisie?"

"I know what the deal is, love. And I'm sorry I drove here alone, at night, but as you can see, I'm perfectly fine."

"Did you tell anyone you were comin'?"

"Well, no, but again, I'm here and I'm okay."

He stepped closer to me, his arms still crossed, his body still closed to me, and I hated it.

I flattened my palms against his chest, the leather of his cut cold to the touch. "I'm okay, honey."

He continued to scowl, but he finally uncrossed his arms and wrapped them around me. "Not happy, Maisie."

"I can see that, love." I slid my arms under his cut and gave him a squeeze. "I'm sorry."

"Fuck!" he growled.

I squeezed my eyes shut and held on tight, then let out a sigh of resignation. "Come with me."

I took his hand and dragged him out of the room, past some very amused looking bikers, and to the back of the compound. As I pushed open the door into the office area of the auto body shop, Hatch flipped on the lights and asked, "Sunshine, what the fuck's goin' on?"

"I have been trying to hide this damn thing for weeks, and quite frankly, it's stressing me out, so you're getting it tonight." He raised an eyebrow and I squeezed his hand. "Close your eyes."

By now, the rest of whoever had been hanging around had followed us into the back.

"Where did you stow it, buddy?" I asked Hawk.

"We put it back here," he said, sounding a little irked, and walked toward the main shop.

Hatch and I followed (along with the rest of the guys).

"You know, we had this," Hawk lamented... again. "If you'd left it alone, this coulda waited."

"It was your job to keep him away from the compound, period," I pointed out. "Excuse me if I had a little less faith in your ability to keep the secret...you know, since he's been here almost every day for a week."

"You really bustin' my balls right now?" Hawk asked.

I sighed. "No. Not really. I appreciate your help. He's impossible, so I know what you were up against."

"Hey now," Hatch said. "What the fuck did I do?"

"Why aren't your eyes closed?"

"Can't follow you if my eyes are closed, Sunshine."

"Well, close them now, please," I said, and kissed him quickly.

He did as I requested, and then Hawk pulled the cover off his surprise.

"You can open them now," I said.

"Are you fuckin' shittin' me?" he virtually squeaked.

"Not even a little bit," I said.

He circled the vintage bike, his expression one of awe. "Is this really a 1928 Indian Hill Climber?"

"Yep," Ace said. "Found it down in Salem, and Mav and I picked it up last month."

"It needs a lot of work," I rushed to say, suddenly feeling a little insecure about my exorbitant purchase. "But you've been saying you wanted a project—"

His mouth was on mine before I could even finish my thought. I slid my hands in his hair as I was lifted high enough to wrap my legs around his waist and promptly carried out of the shop and up the stairs to our private room.

"Hatch," I said between kisses. "The bike—"

"Can wait," he growled, setting me on my feet. "Right now, I'm gonna fuckin' show you my gratitude."

I shivered in anticipation. "I can live with that."

He threw off his cut and pulled off his shirt, while I slid my T-shirt over my head, then unclasped my bra. Licking my lips, I ran my fingers between his pecs. He reached for me, unzipping my jeans and pushing them off my body, panties and all.

"On your back, Sunshine."

"No," I argued and knelt in front of him, unbuttoning his jeans and tugging them down his legs. I wrapped my fingers around his hardening length and slid my hand down, cupping him before taking his cock into my mouth. Hatch hissed, fisting his hands in my hair.

I took him deep in the back of my throat, my mouth watering almost as much as my pussy, and dragged my lips up and down his length, licking the pre-cum off his tip before taking him deep again.

Hatch tugged my hair gently. "On your knees."

I'd learned pretty early on in our relationship that he was in charge in the bedroom, and I was thrilled by his bossiness when it came to sex, so I immediately went there. Hatch guided himself inside of me and I dropped my head back at the sensation.

"So fuckin' wet." His palm connected with my bare bottom and I whimpered and pushed my body back against him.

"Love the bike, baby," he said, burying himself deeper. "Didn't think I could fuckin' love you more."

I didn't get the chance to respond as he slammed into me again, his palm slapping me a little harder this time and the sensation overtook everything. Sliding one hand between my legs and fingering my clit, I came the second the palm of his other hand slapped against my bottom again, crying out while he continued to thrust into me. His body locked and he wrapped his arms around me, gently rolling us to the side and nibbling the back of my neck.

"So, you like the bike," I deduced, and Hatch laughed, turning me to face him.

He stroked my cheek and his eyes got soft as he said, "I love you Maisie Wallace. I'd love you even if you didn't spend a fuckin' mint to buy me that bike, but I do love the bike."

"It wasn't quite a mint," I said.

"You know what I love more, though?"

"What?"

"The fact you went to all those lengths to surprise me." He kissed me gently. "You bring me to my knees, baby. In the best of ways."

"Technically, I was the one on my knees."

He shook his head. "You really can't take a compliment, can you?"

I smiled. "Guilty."

"Not gonna beat a dead horse about you drivin' here, but I need you to promise you won't do that again, sunshine."

"I can do that, darling. I should have trusted Hawk to keep the secret."

"Yeah, baby, you should have."

"But I can't say I regret rushing over here...I'll take a thorough fucking as punishment any day."

Hatch laughed. "I love you."

"I love you, too." I leaned over and kissed him. "And I win."

From our first Christmas together, we'd been competing to out-Christmas Christmas. So far, Hatch had won all but one year, because he was so incredibly sentimental and romantic, and I just wasn't. But this year, I was pretty confident I'd won.

Hatch slid off the bed. "It's not Christmas yet, Sunshine."

I sat up with a shrug. "Doesn't matter. I win."

He grinned as he dragged on his clothing. "You that confident, baby?"

"Well, I *was*." I bit my lip. "What have you done?"

"Me?" he asked, all mock innocence and shit.

I jumped off the bed and slid my arms around his waist. "Did you buy me a pony? Because a pony might give you a lead in the contest, but if it's not a pony, then I win."

He grinned, leaning down to kiss me. "You'll have to wait until Christmas morning."

I wrinkled my nose. "I hate waiting."

"I'm aware…further proven by the fact you couldn't wait to show me my surprise."

I donned my clothes and said, "I *had* to do that."

"Yep, sure you did," he deadpanned.

I gripped his cut and grinned up at him. "That's my story and I'm stickin' to it."

"Doublin' down. I like it." He kissed me again and stroked my neck. "Come on, baby, I'll drive you home. A couple of the recruits can bring my truck back tomorrow."

"Where's the Christmas truck?"

"Safe," he said. "I'll tell you the story on the way home."

I nodded and followed him out of the room, then down to the great room where Hatch spent some time hugging his brothers and thanking them for keeping the secret, then he led me out to my car and took me home…where he thanked me some more.

TIME TO PARTY

*Dani*

THE MORNING OF the party, I woke up with a tightness in my belly and a general uncomfortableness, but I refused to say anything to Austin, because he'd just freak out and overreact. The same thing happened with Archer, and Austin had rushed me to the hospital three times (in less than a week) before the doctor said not to come back unless my contractions were less than five-minutes apart. I thought my man's head would explode...or he'd kill the doctor, so I'd had to keep my pain to myself for several weeks and it wasn't easy.

"Baby, you ready?"

I took a deep breath, and called out, "Yep!"

I ran my hands over my stomach and took another couple of deep breaths before heading down the hall and into the foyer. Austin grinned, holding my coat and helping me into it. Once it was over my shoulders, he placed his hands gently on my belly, leaned down, and kissed me, before standing with a frown. "You're rock hard, baby."

"Am I?"

He raised an eyebrow. "You in pain?"

"No." It wasn't a lie. I wasn't in pain right at that second.

"We should call the doctor."

I smiled, reaching up to stroke his cheek. "Honey, I'm fine. The baby's fine. I promise, I'll take it slow and let other people do the work, okay?"

He continued to study me.

"I'm dying to meet Gator and see all the kids. Don't make me miss it by rushing me to the hospital. It'll just end up being nothing, and a total waste of time."

"Dani—"

"I promise if I feel pain, I'll tell you."

"Dad, we need to go," Cash said.

"I know, bud." Austin sighed, but gave me a reluctant nod. "One twinge and I wanna know about it."

"Deal," I said.

He kissed me again, then we headed downstairs and piled into the truck.

Arriving at the compound, I waddled inside while Austin and the boys grabbed all of the food.

"Dani!" Kim called, rushing to me and pulling me in for a gentle hug. "How are you?"

"The same as I was yesterday when you 'were in the neighborhood' and dropped by to check on me."

She giggled as she guided me to an oversized chair and forced me to sit down. "Macey and Dallas are coming later, so maybe Macey can check you over."

Macey was a registered nurse and just happened to be Payton's bestie.

"Honey, I'm fine," I insisted.

"Awesome," Kim retorted. "She'll be able to confirm that."

"God, lady, you're worse than my husband."

She grinned. "I'll take that as a compliment."

I rolled my eyes, but sank lower in the well-worn chair.

"I'll get you some cider."

"Thanks," I said, just as Austin made his way to me.

He hugged Kim as she passed, then closed the distance between us, leaning down to kiss me gently. "You good?"

"I'm good, honey."

"Prez said Doc's here, so I'm gonna go find him."

Doc was the president of the Savannah Chapter, and had flown in to join in on the festivities. I'd met him a couple of times over the past few years and I really liked him. One day, I hoped I'd actually make it to Savannah and meet the rest of the guys there…the clubhouse sounded insane and I was dying to see it.

Doc and Hatch had been buddies for a while, and Doc had apparently brought his Sgt. At Arms, Alamo, with him. They were only here for a couple of days, so I had a feeling more might be going on. If there was, however, it would be considered club business, so it was none of mine.

"Okay, honey."

He kissed me again and then headed toward the kitchen.

"Is Santa coming now?" Jagger asked as he made a run for me.

I held my arms out and scooped him onto my lap. "Soon, baby."

"Jagger," Kim admonished gently, returning with some warm cider for me. "Aunty can't have you climbing all over her, baby."

"He's fine," I countered. "I always need some Jagger love."

He grinned big and kissed my cheek, but still climbed off my lap and joined my kids who were checking out the presents under the tree. I took the cider from Kim and she sat on the sofa next to my chair. "Did you see Doc?" I asked.

She nodded. "Yeah. I was mobbed by all the single ladies trying to get to him."

"He's pretty sexy." I chuckled. "You didn't hear that from me, though."

"Of course not…even though I agree." She glanced around the room, then leaned in and whispered, "Just wait until you see Alamo, though. Lord-eeee, the man is *fine*."

Before I could comment, the man walked in the room. I knew it was Alamo; A, because I'd never met him before, and, B, because he walked in with Doc and the room seemed to quiet. Mostly because all female eyes were on the newcomers.

Kim wasn't kidding about Alamo. He was all lean muscle, dark hair, longish on top, and a beard that rivaled Hatch's. When he smiled, his blue eyes lit up and I swore I heard a chorus of female sighs echo through the room.

"Where's this Gator guy?" I asked Kim.

"He's changing. He's playing Santa."

"Oh, that's sweet." I frowned. "Wait, is he using the suit he stole?"

Kim giggled. "Yep. Duke didn't want it back."

"I don't blame him."

Because Gator had been staying at the homeless shelter, Crow had made the decision to open up the compound for the kids staying there, so they would be arriving in less than an hour, would be fed and each kid would get a gift from "Santa." I couldn't wait.

And neither could the kids.

The next three hours were spent laughing and eating, along with watching the little kids fawn over Santa. Well, the ones that weren't screaming in fear, that is.

Gator was amazing. I knew he'd had a rough go of it over the last year, but he was born to be around kids. He loved it and they loved him. He looked like Sam Elliott and Tom Selleck had a love child, and he was gorgeous.

"How are you feeling?" Kim asked me, and I smiled up at her.

"I feel good," I lied.

She frowned just as a sharp pain rolled through my belly.

"Dani?"

I swallowed. "Get Austin. My water just broke."

"Holy shit," she whispered, then turned and bellowed, "Booker! Dani's havin' your baby."

"I hadn't planned on this being a group thing, Kimmie," I grumbled.

Austin rushed toward me, Doc behind him. "Baby?"

"My water broke," I said.

Doc leaned over me. "Do you mind if I feel your belly?"

I shook my head and he checked me over just as Macey walked up with a stethoscope. Doc took it and listened, then smiled. "Let's get this mama to the hospital."

Austin helped me up and I groaned.

"What, baby?"

"I'm not going to make it to the hospital," I rasped. "This little girl is coming now."

"Get her up to your room, Booker," Macey said. "We'll call an ambulance while we try to keep the baby inside."

"No, you don't understand," I countered, grabbing for Austin. "She's coming. Right now."

Austin swept me up into his arms and carried me to the bunk room which on the first floor. Doc, Macey, and Kim followed, and I bent over in pain when Austin set me on my feet.

"Let's get her out of those wet clothes," Doc said. "We called for an ambulance, but it's gonna take a little while for it to get here."

Macey pulled a comforter off one of the beds and doubled it over to throw on the sofa while Austin helped me out of my wet bottoms.

Easing me down onto the sofa, Macey covered me with a sheet while Doc washed his hands and donned gloves. While he got me into a good position, Macey washed her hands and grabbed gloves so that she could assist.

"I can see the head," Doc said, and smiled up at me. "You ready to have this baby?"

I reached for Austin. "Are the kids okay?"

"Payton and Maisie have the kids under control, and Cass and Darien are covering clean-up, so you just worry about you and the baby," Kim said. "Okay?"

Austin smiled at my best friend. "Thanks, babe."

I groaned as a contraction hit and then my body decided it was time to push. It took about twelve minutes and four pushes to deliver our baby girl and I cried the second I had her in my arms.

"Ohmigod, she's perfect," I whispered as I

counted her fingers and toes and kissed her forehead. Glancing up at Austin, he gave me his nod of approval, so I focused back on our daughter.

"Daisy May Carver, welcome to the world, sweet girl."

"Oh my god, that's so cute!" Kim said, and clapped her hands.

Austin didn't speak as he leaned down to kiss Daisy, then me, just as the EMTs arrived. As I was loaded onto a gurney, Daisy and I were wrapped in a blanket together and wheeled through the great room where our family congratulated us as we passed by.

"We've got the kids covered," Kim said. "We'll bring them by later."

"Thanks, honey."

I let tears fall as we were loaded into the ambulance and driven to where we'd ultimately be told how textbook and perfect the delivery had gone, and how lucky I was to have such a skilled medical team so close. Lucky didn't even begin to cover it.

My world was filled with perfection and pure joy.

EPILOGUE

*Maisie*

## Christmas Eve

**M**ACK AND DARIEN were the last to arrive for our little "nucleus" get-to-gether. Because the majority of us lived within walking distance of each other, we always made Christmas Eve our "family time." The rest of our little group were already partying it up in the family room, including Dani and Daisy, who was now ten days old.

"Come in," I said, waving the little family inside. "Harper and Ryan, all the other kids are downstairs if you want to go play. I have it on good authority that Flash has even set up the karaoke machine."

"Whoo-hoo!" Harper squealed, dropping her coat and shoes in the middle of the foyer and dragging her sister downstairs.

Darien groaned, cleaning up the discarded mess. "Sorry, Maisie."

"Let her go have fun," I said, taking the coats and hanging them up. "You can make them mind their manners at your house."

Mack smiled. "Thanks, babe."

"Come on in. Cassidy's already on her third nog. Damn, that girl is funny when she's tipsy."

"Right?" Darien said with a laugh.

"Shit, is that Minus?" Mack asked.

I nodded. Hatch's sister, Cricket, had been 'shackin' up with the outlaw' for years, and although Hatch respected him (sort of), he didn't like the idea of his baby sister 'givin' away the milk for free.' But Minus had surprised Cricket with an engagement ring on her birthday, so Hatch had decided to put his distrust of Minus aside for the moment.

What my husband didn't realize, was the holdout for marriage had never been Minus...it was all Cricket. Those of us in the know, however, kept that little tidbit of information to ourselves. Because if we didn't, Hatch would handcuff her and Minus and the nearest preacher, priest, or justice of the peace he could find.

"Darien!" Cassidy called, setting her glass on the coffee table and making an unsteady walk toward her. "You look amazing."

She hugged Cassidy while I grabbed Mack and Darien drinks.

Darien shook her head. "Um, I can't actually drink."

"Are you sick?"

She smiled. "Nope."

"Ohmigod! You're pregnant," Payton squealed and jumped from her place on Hawk's lap to hug her.

"I am," Darien confirmed, laying her hands on her stomach. "We're really hoping for a boy."

We descended upon the couple en-masse, hugging them, before Darien insisted on holding the new addition who was sleeping on Austin's chest.

"Good luck prying her away from Daddy," Dani said. "He's stingy with the Daisy love."

Darien held her arms out and flapped her hands. "Gimmie, Book."

Booker reluctantly handed Daisy over to Darien who settled her on her chest and crooned while the baby continued to sleep.

"Did Gator settle in okay?" Mack asked as Hatch pulled me onto his lap in one of our over-stuffed chairs.

"Yeah. He's apparently lovin' Savannah," Hatch said. "I say we all head out there this summer. Road trip."

Gator had decided he needed a change, and Doc had offered him a place at the Savannah chapter where he'd help him stay clean and give him a job. Gator said he was sick of the rain and jumped at the chance.

"Hell, yeah," Mack said. "I'm in."

As I snuggled closer to my man, the light caught my early Christmas gift, and I couldn't stop myself from staring at it. My grandmother had given me a ring, years ago, that had seen better days, but I adored it…partly because it was from my Gran, but partly because it had a sunshine pattern which took on new meaning when I fell in love with Hatch.

Unbeknownst to me, he took it in to a jeweler and had several of the tiny diamonds replaced, along with the middle stone (which he replaced with my birthstone…a stunning sapphire). When it was finished and cleaned up, it was even better than the original. In the end, I'd had to admit he might have come very close to winning this round…very close. Hatch gave me a gentle squeeze and I kissed him, then we continued to drink and make merry until the kitchen timer went off to signal dinner was ready.

Because our men all cooked, they were the ones who headed into the kitchen to carve and prep the rest of the meal, while we gathered the kids and got everyone washed up and seated at the table.

Hatch sat at the head of our giant table and raised his glass of whiskey. "May your turkeys get basted and all your stockings be stuffed."

"Connor," I admonished, even though I was trying desperately to keep from laughing.

He grinned. "Okay, okay. Love all of you weirdos. Let's eat!"

We dissolved into laughter as we slayed dinner, then put a serious dent in our liquor cabinet, and I beamed at my husband who'd brought so much happiness to my life.

Our road had led to joy, and I couldn't have been more grateful.

# MINUS

BURNING SAINTS MC BOOK #1

# JACK DAVENPORT

Unedited Excerpt ©2018 Trixie Publishing, Inc.

# PROLOGUE
*Minus*

*DON'T PASS OUT.*
The pain in my head was blinding, I couldn't focus on anything in the room, and began to drift into darkness.

*Don't pass out.*
I forced my eyes open just as I felt another blow from the phonebook. My vision blurred and a wave of nausea hit me. I tried to stay as lucid as possible, focusing on anything around me that may help me escape. I had to stay sharp if I was going to find a way out of this. My host had been letting his fingers do the walking upside my head for some time now, and I wasn't going to be able to hold out much longer.

*Don't fucking pass out.*
"Come on hero, don't make me beat you to death. This could all end right now if you just tell me what I need to know." His words swam in my

head, barely cutting through the ringing in my ears.

It took every ounce of strength I had to form the necessary response, "All you need to know…is that…you hit…like a bitch." I spit blood and bits of my fractured molar onto his boots.

Another blow, this time to the back of my head, and it felt like he's taken a running start this time. My chin connected with sternum and every muscle in my neck burned from the whiplash.

"He said you'd be tough, and he was right," my torturer said. "He also said you'd be mouthy."

*I'm sure… he did.*

"I'd agree with him there," he continued, wiping sweat from his brow. "But he also said, you were smart, and that I'm just not buyin' that. You see, if you were smart, you'd tell me where the girl and the book are."

"It seems you… have me at a disadvantage, sir," I said, my words slurred. "You seem to know so much about me, but I know… so little about you." I paused and then smiled wide. "Other than the obvious fact that you're a dickless rodent that can only get off when you're torturing people and fantasizing about having sex with your sister."

He must really have a sister because I felt the full impact of the phonebook, from AAA Carpet Cleaners to the Zywicki family. The chair I was tied to toppled over, and the zip ties that bound me cut deep into my wrists with searing pain. The side of my already pummeled head hit the floor, and within seconds I was out like a light.

When I came to, I was once again sitting upright, but was no longer tied to the chair. In fact, I wasn't in a chair at all. I was in the passenger seat of a car that was hauling ass through the Portland night.

"Hang on! Stay with me!"

As soon as I heard her voice, I smiled. It probably looked more like a deranged grin given the current state of my face, but I couldn't help it.

Once again, she'd found me, and once again she'd saved my life.

# CHAPTER ONE
*Minus*

*One month earlier...*

"THIS IS BAD news."

"Well, hello to you, too," I said as I shoved my duffel bag into the back of Clutch's '71 Barracuda. He'd restored it by hand to its original condition. It was his pride and joy, and everyone in town knew it.

"Watch the interior, you fuckin' hick, and if you've got any of that shit tucked in your lip, you'd better spit it out before you get in," he said.

"Fuck you," I replied as I slid into my seat.

"Hey, man, how am I supposed to know what kind of shit you're into these days? Just look at you! You're wearing fucking cowboy boots. For all I know, you're carrying a six shooter under your jacket," he said, pulling away from the curb and into the flow of airport traffic.

"From what I've heard, all of Portland is in beards and cowboy boots these days," I replied.

"Yeah, a lot has changed since you've been gone. Then again," he paused, "a lot of shit is *exactly* the same," he said, throwing me sideways glance.

I said nothing, but we both knew very well what he meant. When I left town six years ago it wasn't under the best circumstances, to say the least.

"Don't get me wrong, brother, it's great to see you back home—"

"This isn't home," I interrupted.

"Which leads me back to my original point," he replied. "It can only be bad news that the not-so-prodigal son is back in town."

"Please, brother, this warm welcome is all just a little too much. You're gonna embarrass me."

"Don't get cute with me, motherfucker, you know exactly what I'm saying," he replied.

"Oh, believe me, I know all too well. In Savannah I'm a Yankee and here I'm a redneck. I'm a man without a country, but here I am, nonetheless."

"Yeah, but *why* are you here?" Clutch asked.

"Because Cutter asked me to be here."

"See! Bad fuckin' news!" Clutch exclaimed.

"How is that bad news?"

"Since when is it *not* bad news when the Prez sends for you?"

I laughed. "*Sends* for you? What are we, wiseguys? He called me, and asked me to get on the next plane to Portland, so here I am. To be honest, I thought you'd know what's going on, being the new Sargent—"

"Don't you fuckin' start with me, Minus."

"Sargent Clutch. Ooooh, that does have a nice ring to it."

"I'll kick you right to the fucking curb and you can walk the rest of the way," he deadpanned.

"Hey man, in all seriousness, congratulations. It's a big deal, you making Sargent at Arms, and I'm proud of you."

"Thanks, man. We all miss Rusty, but after he died the club needed someone to step up, and I guess Cutter thought it should be me."

"I'm sure he was right," I said.

"Bullshit. You know goddamned well if you were still in town, it'd be you wearing the Sargent patch."

"Well, then it's a good for you I'm not still in town."

Clutch and I grew up together in Portland, back when I still went by my given name, he was known as Nicky, and together we were known as trouble. We were both orphans who had been taken in, and educated by the Catholic church. A handful of us kids were fortunate to receive scholarships to private schools in the Portland area, and Nicky and I attended St. Mary's Academy together; that is, until he was kicked out during our sophomore year. I loved school, especially anything to do with reading. I inhaled novels, biographies, textbooks, anything I could get my hands on. I found it easy to make friends and blended in with the crowd wherever we went. Nikolai Christakos, not so much.

Coming up in Portland in the "naughties," Nicky had two things going against him. First of all, he was Greek. These days Portland is more of a melting pot; with a sort-of 'college town' vibe where just about anybody can do their thing, but this was not the case back in the day. Portland was still pretty dominated by a culture of white boy, blue collar types. Nicky was dark skinned, but not black, tough, but not into sports, anti-social, but not a loner.

To put it mildly, he didn't fit in anywhere, and him being Greek somehow seemed to be the central cause of this. Secondly, Nicky would fight anybody, and mean anybody; Teachers, students, cops, hell, I saw him take a swing at a priest once. Unfortunately for Nicky, that priest was a former golden gloves boxing champ. He'd also apparently not read the "turn the other cheek" part of the Bible in seminary and hit Nicky with a stiff jab, causing blood to pour from his nose.

This kind of thing was simply commonplace where we came up. I on the other hand, got along with just about everybody in the neighborhood, and always looked out for Nicky. I made sure he came with me to parties and football games. The kinds of places where young people meet other young people. I thought it would be good for him, but without fail, some jackass would mouth off to him, or he'd hit on someone's girl, and then it was on. Bloody lips, loose teeth and black eyes seemed to follow him wherever he went, so eventually the school kicked him out, the church had enough, and he was out on the street. I was his only friend and I knew that if he was out on his own, he'd get himself arrested, beat up or killed within weeks, so I left school, and he and I moved to downtown Portland together.

Being broke, we bought bikes to get around town, which lead to fixing bikes, which eventually lead us to the Burning Saints Motorcycle Club and our current lives as Minus and Clutch.

"Hey man…ah, we've got a quick stop to make before we go to the clubhouse," Clutch said. I could tell by the shift in his tone that I wasn't going to like where we were headed, and I was right.

* * *

*Cricket*

"Don't Even think about it, asshole!" I yelled out to the motorist attempting to merge into our lane. My Uber driver flinched and reflexively cupped his right ear. "Don't take your hand off the wheel, you're gonna let him in! Don't let him in!"

I was a fraction of a second away from grabbing the steering wheel, and literally attempting to back-seat drive, when my long-suffering coachman shot me a look, and said sternly, "Lady, if you're going to do that again, I'm going to have to let you out at the nearest safe stopping place."

"I'm sorry," I grumbled. "I really am, I'm just very—"

"Late," he finished my sentence. "Yes, I know. You've explained this *many* times since I picked you up."

He'd clearly lost patience with me, and I couldn't blame him. This poor guy was just trying to do his job and I was sucking him into my vortex of chaos.

"I'm so sorry, it's just that I'm meeting with someone I haven't seen in a really long time, and

I'm not even sure why I agreed to meet with him, and I know it's going to get me into trouble with my brother who's being a big jerk, but I know he's just trying to protect me, but I don't want his protection, and I hate being late," I said, sheepishly pausing to take a deep breath, now embarrassed by my outburst.

"Hey, it's okay. I've got a brother and he's an asshole, too, what can you do?"

"My brother's as far from an asshole as you can get," I snapped.

"Sorry."

I sighed. "No, it's okay. I sound like a bitch… or a lunatic. Omigod, I sound like a lunatic bitch. I'm so sorry."

I was even more nervous than I thought. I hated that my older brother, Hatch, could still make me feel like a little girl. I knew he was going to be furious with me, and I suppose he'd have good reason, but I still didn't like the fact that soon he'd likely be sitting me down and scolding me for making decisions that were *mine* to make. I'm an adult and I didn't need his permission or blessing to visit a family member if I wanted to. It's true that he's had to act more like a father than a brother to me, and the fact that he's seventeen years older makes it worse, but I really wondered if there was ever going to be a time when he'd start treating me like an adult; like his equal.

*But what the hell does my uncle want?*

When I was a little girl, my dad, my uncle, and their buddy Crow used to ride with the Dogs of Fire motorcycle club in San Diego. They'd been asked by the club's president to start a new chapter in Portland and we were all going to move, but then my mother got sick and everything changed overnight. When she died, my dad went off the rails, and eventually ended up in prison.

My uncle and Crow went to Portland as planned, but it seems they had very different ideas of what a motorcycle club should look like. Crow stayed with the Dogs of Fire, and over time, became the club's national president. My uncle, however, along with a small group of dirt bags and petty criminals, started the Burning Saints. Since then, I'd seen very little of my uncle over the years, so why in God's name I've been asked to meet with him is anyone's guess.

"Okay, here we are," my driver said as we reached our destination. I could swear he was trying to hide the sound of relief in his voice.

"Thank you again, and sorry for the…um…backseat driving. I promise I'll leave you a glowing review," I said, slinking out of car.

Moments later I found myself standing in front of a place I never thought I'd be, and took a deep breath before opening the door.

\* \* \*

*Minus*

"What the fuck is in this coffee, Phil?"

"I'm sorry, Clutch, I would have made a fresh pot if I knew you guys were...stopping by. Here let me make..."

Phil tried to stand, but the barrel of Clutch's gun pointed at his head convinced him to remain seated.

"You're good right there, Phil. I'm just going sit here and sip my *delicious* cup of motor oil, while my good friend Minus looks for Cutter's money."

I shot a cold stare back at Clutch, who was now in full on 'Sargent at Arms Mode.' He was clearly the perfect choice for the position.

"Really, it's no trouble, Clutch. I'm happy to do it." Heavy beads of sweat formed on Phil's stubbled upper lip, which was frozen in a permanent nervous grin.

"You see, that's always been your problem, Phil, you don't listen very well. For instance, you didn't listen when I told you not to bother with the coffee. We won't be here for very long, and highly I doubt the next cup could possibly be any better than this swill." Clutch dumped the remainder of his cup on Phil's trash littered desk. "You also failed to hear me when I asked you where Cutter's money is, and now my associate, Minus, is probably going to get his nice expensive cowboy boots dirty rooting around your filthy shop looking for it.

I flipped Clutch off and began casually tossing Phil's rat hole of an office. It wasn't as his place was some sort of secured facility. His shitty garage was on par with who he was, a low-level guy that Cutter used only when needed.

"I doubt even Phil would be stupid enough to keep that much money here," I said.

"Are you, Phil?" Clutch asked.

"What?" Phil asked.

"Are you that stupid?"

"What?"

"You keep saying what. Are you having trouble with your hearing, Phil? Maybe I can help you with that."

Clutch holstered his gun and pulled out a blade. He walked behind Phil and grabbed his head, his knife to his ear. He tried to squirm, but Clutch's hold was firm.

"This is a chop-shop after all; a place where very large things get cut up into very small pieces, so this should work out pretty well. I'm going to ask you one more time to point us in the direction of Cutter's two million dollars. If you fail to hear me this time, I'm going to be forced to improve your hearing."

I chuckled. "Wouldn't cutting his ear off make his hearing worse?"

"I'm not a doctor, Minus. I'm pretty sure Phil here understands that I'm doing the best I can under the circumstances, don't you, Phil?"

Phil's bloodshot eyes bulged from their sockets, as he grunted out, "Sure Clutch."

"I'm just doing the best I can to help my good buddy Phil hear my question as clearly as possible. So here it goes, one more time. Where is Cutter's fucking money?"

"It's not here…"

The first drops of blood appeared as the blade pressed into the soft flesh where his earlobe connected to his head.

"I'll tell you where it is!" he screamed. "I swear to God I'll tell you where it is."

Clutch stopped, straightened up, and he looked at me smiling. "See, it worked! He can hear just fine now.

"I think you missed your calling, *Doctor* Clutch," I said.

"You asshole, you almost cut my fucking ear off!" Phil snapped.

"*Almost* being the operative word, Philly Cheese Steak. Now, where is the money?" Clutch asked, once again leveling his pistol to Phil's head.

"A dude named Viper hired my crew to steal a car. That's it!" he squeaked. "I swear I didn't know there was money in the trunk until the car got here, and they opened it up."

"But once you saw the money, you didn't think to call Cutter?"

"How was I supposed to know the money was his?"

"Don't make me shoot you just for being stupid, Phil. You knew that two million was coming in for the Saints. Everyone in the Club's circle knew about the payment, and that includes you. You should have called him as soon as you saw the cash."

"You're right, Clutch. You're absolutely right." Blood ran down the rolls of pink flesh that were his neck as his hands applied pressure to the wound.

I cocked my head. "Now tell me, who the fuck is Viper and where can I find him?"

"He's the head of Los Psychos, the Mexican club. They hang out at the Nine Ball."

"The pool hall?"

"That's the place! I swear that's all I know. It was just supposed to be a simple job; snatch the car, and bring it back here for pickup. I didn't know anything about Cutter's money being in the trunk, or that you were involved Minus." Phil's attention turned to me. "Last I heard you moved to Texas or something."

"Savannah, Georgia," I replied dryly. "Now leave me the fuck out of this." I'd always hated Phil. He was a piece of shit and I couldn't wait to get out of here. Besides being a car thief, Phil was also a loan shark and meth dealer. The exact sort of person I was trying to protect my club from years ago.

Phil continued, "I know Cutter and I have had our disagreements lately…and that mistakes have been made. Like I said, I didn't know it was his money and I will *personally* apologize to Cutter myself."

"Don't worry, Phil, I'll let him know you were sorry."

Phil's body, now two holes greater, lie on his office floor in a heap, a pool of blood rapidly forming underneath his lumpy frame.

Clutch, huffed in irritation.

"What the fuck, man?" I shouted

"Cutter wanted him gone," Clutch said flatly.

"You didn't want to clue me in? I would have brought my kit."

"No time. I've got a cleaning crew on standby. Cutter wants this all taken care of right away. We still have to find this Viper prick, and I'd like to be in bed before three a.m."

"No, *you* need to find Viper," I snapped back. "I'm only here for a meeting with Cutter and that's it. I'm here for twenty-four hours and then I'm headed back to Savannah. As a matter of fact, I'm not even here."

"Yeah, well plans may have just changed," he said as he dialed the number for the cleaning crew.

"Yes, I called earlier about a bad stain in my carpet," Clutch said. "That's correct, the one located in my hallway. I'd like to have a crew come out right away please. Thank you."

He hung up and we and I made our way out through the back entrance, to his car which was parked in the rear lot. As we got in, Clutch said, "Ya know, you still haven't told me exactly why you're back in town."

"I already told fuckin' told you, Cutter called me and asked me to meet with him, so here I am."

"I understand that, but *why?*" he asked as we peeled off into the night. "Everyone here thought you were swallowed up by the south, as the late great Phil so astutely pointed out."

"*Astutely?*" I choked out in surprise.

"Hey, motherfucker, I read some of those books you sent me when I was in the joint. Anyways, don't change the subject."

"I told you I have no idea, and I wouldn't lie to you, now slowdown, will ya? The last thing we need is for your dumb ass to be get pulled over fleeing a murder scene."

Clutch barely slowed down as he continued his interrogation, "Don't get cute with me, bro. Maybe it's just me, but it seems a little odd that you're so casual about meeting with a guy that you haven't spoken directly to in six years, exiled you to Hicksville USA, and that…Oh yeah, once tried to kill you!

"Look, you know Cutter as well as I do. He never does anything without good reason. He has his reasons for asking me here, and I have my reasons for saying yes."

"Is one of those reasons her?" he challenged.

"Fuck you, Nicky."

"That's not a no."

"Actually, it's a fuck you, Nicky. I haven't talked to her in six years, and she has no idea that

I'm in town. In fact, no one knows I'm in town and that's exactly the way I want to keep it."

"Well, Phil sure as fuck knows," Clutch said laughing. "I've gotta feeling Viper's gonna know pretty soon as well."

"I told you you're on your own with this bullshit. I don't know anything about Cutter's two million dollars, or who this Viper guy is, but it definitely sounds like more of a *you* problem, than a *me* problem," I said.

Clutch's expression turned deadly serious. "It's a club problem, Minus, and last I checked, you still wear a Saints patch."

I nodded, but said nothing. We drove on through the ever-present Portland drizzle until we reached the clubhouse.

"Trust me, Minus, as important as you may *think* you are to Cutter, the club's two million in cash is more important," Clutch said as he parked. "I'm gonna have to sniff around a little and see what we can find out about Viper and his crew. For all we know, Phil was lying through his rotten teeth, but Cutter's gonna want me to make sure, and honestly, I could use some trustworthy backup, so are you gonna help me with this or not?"

I paused for few moments then asked, "Who's the two million from?"

"Honestly, I don't know. Cutter's been cagey lately; really secretive and shit. He's been keeping everyone at arm's length, so I don't think it's a coincidence that you've been summoned to be here, at the same time that this payment was scheduled to be delivered."

"I told you, I have no idea why I'm here Clutch."

"I believe you, man, I just don't believe that you haven't thought about what you might say or do if you see… *her*."

"You can say her name ya know. You can say Cricket."

"*I* can say her name, but *you* can't, my friend. According to Cutter you can't see her, talk to her, say her name, or even think about her."

"Yeah, he made that pretty clear the night he hung me over the Burnside bridge, so why the fuck do you keep bringing her up?"

We got out of the car and made our way to the entrance.

"Just making sure you've got your head on straight should you run into her that's all," Clutch said, his hand on the front door.

"Being as she and Cutter don't talk, she and I don't talk, and Cutter and I don't talk, I can't imagine why or how I could possibly run into Cricket Wallace," I said.

Clutch opened the door and it took me a moment to believe what I was seeing.

Strawberry blonde hair, long legs that supported the sexiest body ever created, and a face that was so beautiful that it made me forget what any other woman I'd ever seen looked like.

Cricket Wallace was standing ten feet away from me, in the middle of the Saint's clubhouse.

"Hi, Jase, it's good to see you again."

ABOUT PIPER

Piper Davenport writes from a place of passion and intrigue, combining elements of romance and suspense with strong modern-day heroes and heroines.

She currently resides in pseudonymia under the dutiful watch of the Writers Protection Agency.

Like Piper's FB page and get to know her!
(www.facebook.com/piperdavenport)

Twitter: @piper_davenport
Sign up for her mailing list!

81231785R00076

Made in the USA
Columbia, SC
26 November 2017